GOD THE ULTIMATE SUPERHERO

by **Alicia Johnson**

Illustrations by Mike Motz

*For my amazing husband and best friend, Jerome.
Son, Bryce, whose curiosity inspired this journey.
Mom, ultimate friend, and encourager.*

*Special thanks to my friend,
Teri Perry—editor extraordinaire.*

GOD
THE ULTIMATE
SUPERHERO

by **Alicia Johnson**

Illustrations by Mike Motz

Published by God Centered Family

Ryan ran into the kitchen with a red superhero cape trailing behind him. "Mom!"

Mom looked up from the cup of hot coffee she was stirring. "Well, hello my little superhero! What's going on?"

Ryan stood in front of his mom. "The book I'm reading says that God is everywhere. Is that true?" Ryan handed the book to his mom. "Yes, Ryan, it is," she replied, pausing to look through the book. "God is everywhere."

Ryan thought carefully about the possibility of God being many places at the same time. Slowly, he began to frown because he was thinking so hard.

"Do you understand how God can be several different places at the same time?" Mom asked, interrupting Ryan's thoughts.

"Impressive observation, Ryan!" Mom said. "I can't think of any superhero that can be everywhere at once. It's amazing how superheroes have some of the greatest powers in the world, but even they can't be more than one place at a time."

Holding the book tightly in both arms, she continued, "Only one God exists, and since He is the only one who can be many places at one time, God must be better than a superhero!"

Ryan sat down; he was determined to prove to his mom that nobody was better than a superhero. "God may have superheroes beat when it comes to being everywhere at once, but He's no match for their superhuman strength!" Ryan clenched his fist and flexed his muscles before continuing. "Superheroes are strong and tough."

Mom chuckled and placed the book on the counter. "You're right. Superheroes are very strong. But if you compare God's strength to a superhero's, it's . . . well, there's no comparison."

Mom took a quick sip of coffee. "See, superheroes might use their strength to fight off villains or crash through buildings, but God doesn't just use His strength. **He *is* our strength** and acts as a shield for us."

Her eyes lit up with excitement. "God even goes a step further and gives us strength when we are tired and power when we are weak! I don't know any superhero who can do that!"

Ryan leaned back in his chair. As hard as he tried, he couldn't think of any superhero who even came close to fitting his mom's description of God, but he wasn't ready to give up yet. "God giving us strength sounds good and all, but what if all the superheroes in the world joined forces and combined their strengths and powers together? Then would superheroes be more powerful than God?"

Mom placed her hand on Ryan's shoulder. "No, not a chance," she answered confidently. "Most superheroes have a limited amount of power, but God is able to do more than we could ever ask or think. **God's power is unlimited,** which is why He's called omnipotent!"

"Hmm, that's interesting," Ryan said. "So if superheroes are no match for the strength and power of God, how does God stack up against superheroes when we think about peace and protection?"

Mom smiled. "I thought you would never ask! Superheroes are excellent crime fighters." She stood up and pretended to fight off evil villains. "They quickly stop the bad guys and restore peace and order, but crime and chaos are no match for God."

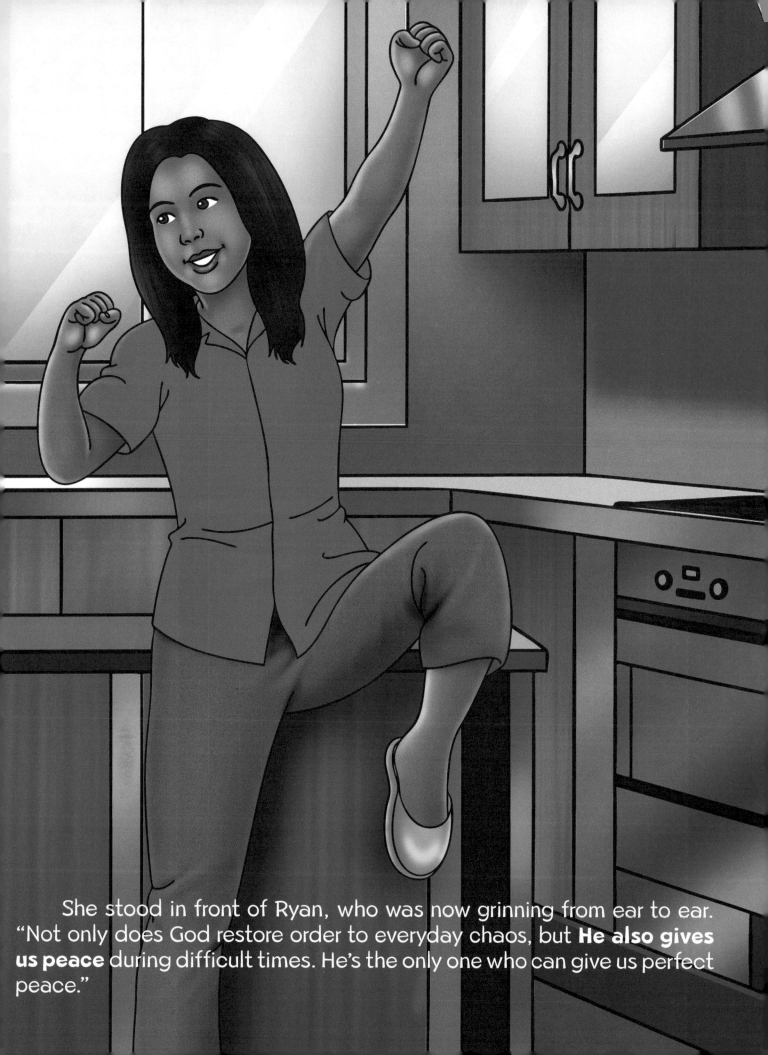

She stood in front of Ryan, who was now grinning from ear to ear. "Not only does God restore order to everyday chaos, but **He also gives us peace** during difficult times. He's the only one who can give us perfect peace."

"But what about a distress call?" Ryan said. "Some of the greatest superheroes wait for a signal to know when they're needed. People use these signals to tell the superheroes that something is wrong. If God is better than a superhero, why doesn't He have his own distress signal?"

"Good question! Let's search your book for the answer. This book tells countless stories of how God stepped into what seemed like impossible situations and rescued people who really, really needed a miracle."

She opened the book and scanned the pages. "The stories mentioned here all have one thing in common: none of the people sent a distress signal to God when they were in need, but God, being who He is, still saw them and rescued them.

It's the same for you and me today. We can call on God at any moment and feel confident knowing that He will answer us. He is already aware of what's going on in our lives. In fact, He knows what's going to happen before it happens."

Mom set the book in front of Ryan. "And that's why God is better than a superhero!"

Ryan took a deep breath and thought about his mother's words and the conversation they'd just had. "Mom was right all along," Ryan thought to himself.

God could run circles around all the superheroes he had read about and watched on television. He was more real than any superhero featured in a comic book. "God *is* better than a superhero. He's the ultimate superhero!" Ryan whispered.

He grabbed the book and quickly flipped through the first few pages. He became more excited with each passing moment.

Mom asked, "What are you looking for?"

Ryan couldn't contain his excitement. "Yes! Here it is!" he shouted pointing to the page. "It says that we are all made in God's image!" Ryan marveled at the text before continuing. "And since God is better than a superhero, then I must be too!"

CPSIA information can be obtained
at www.ICGtesting.com
Printed in the USA
BVHW020425170920
588928BV00003B/177